Walt Disn

Mickey Mouse Flies the Christmas Mail

Told by Annie North Bedford
Illustrated by the Walt Disney Studio
Adapted by Julius Svendsen and Neil Boyle

Everybody loves Mickey Mouse! Even at the
North Pole, where Mickey's latest adventure
takes him, Mickey finds some fur-clad elves who
are ready to help him deliver the Christmas mail.

🌸 A Golden Book • New York

Copyright © 1956, 2007 Disney Enterprises, Inc. All rights reserved. Published in the United States
by Golden Books, an imprint of Random House Children's Books, a division of Random House, Inc.,
New York, and in Canada by Random House of Canada Limited, Toronto, in conjunction with
Disney Enterprises, Inc. GOLDEN BOOKS, A GOLDEN BOOK, A LITTLE GOLDEN BOOK, the G colophon,
and the distinctive gold spine are registered trademarks of Random House, Inc.

www.goldenbooks.com   www.randomhouse.com/kids/disney

Educators and librarians, for a variety of teaching tools, visit us at www.randomhouse.com/teachers

Library of Congress Control Number: 2007922463

ISBN: 978-0-7364-2424-0

Printed in the United States of America

10 9 8 7 6 5 4 3 2

First Random House Edition 2007

Mickey Mouse hung onto the control stick of his little plane as the big wind spun it about.

"Whew!" said Mickey to himself. "I can see why they don't use many of these little planes any more for flying the mail. This wind is stronger than the plane."

Mickey had not expected to be out in the storm on Christmas Eve. He had planned to be safe at home with Minnie Mouse and Morty and Ferdie, their nephews.

They would all read a Christmas story together and
hang up their stockings by the fireplace and go off early to
bed. That was Mickey's plan. But then the airport called.

"Mickey," said the man at the airport, "we're in a jam. The big mail plane is delayed. It won't stop here. We have a big load of Christmas mail. Could you fly it out for us?"

Mickey thought of all that Christmas mail lying at
the airport over Christmas. He thought of the mothers
and daddies and children waiting for it.

"Of course," he said. So he bundled up and said
good-by to Minnie and the boys. And away he went.

Now here he was in his little plane, being blown about by this biggest of all Christmas Eve storms.

He tried to work his radio. But no "beep-beep" radio beam came through. He rubbed his hand across the window. There was nothing to be seen but blowing snow.

"Not a sign of a light below," said Mickey to himself. "I guess I've been blown way off my course. Wonder where in the world I am?"

Mickey got out his compass. "At least the needle will point north," he thought. "I'll know which way I'm flying." But the needle of the compass did not point at all. It spun around as fast as it could. And it seemed to want to point straight down.

"That's funny," said Mickey. "It doesn't seem to be broken. But the way it's acting, to make any sense I'd have to be—why, I'd have to be right over the North Pole!"

Just then the wind began to die down. The snow flakes fell away from Mickey's window. He could see a great stretch of snow below him now. And in the middle of the snow field lights were shining, as bright as the stars in the sky.

"Well," said Mickey. And he sighed with relief. "It's about time. My gas is almost gone. Guess I'd better land on that smooth snow."

So down glided Mickey, as neat as you please, to a three-point landing on the snow.

Before he could open the door of the plane, little figures came running from the lighted house. They were not men but round little elves, all dressed in warm furry suits.

"Welcome!" they cried, "whoever you are." Then as
Mickey stepped out into their lantern beams, they all
cried together, "Why, it's Mickey Mouse!"

Mickey was certainly surprised at that.

"How did you know?" he cried. "Who are you? And
where am I, if I may ask?"

"Who are we?" The little elves chuckled and laughed. "Why, we're Santa Claus's elves, of course. And where are you? Why, you're at the North Pole. And there is Santa Claus's house."

Then they led him over the crunchy, sparkling snow, right up to Santa Claus's door. And there was Mrs. Santa Claus herself, waiting to welcome him.

"Come right in, Mickey Mouse," she said, "and sit down here beside the fire. I'll bring you some cookies and milk."

"Thank you," said Mickey, "I guess I could stop a moment. But I must fill the plane with gas and be on my way again. I have a load of Christmas mail to deliver tonight, you see."

"Gas?" said the elves. And their smiles faded. "Dear, dear, we have none of that here."

"But how about Santa Claus's old sleigh, boys?" Mrs. Santa Claus asked. "And all the retired reindeer are out in the barn. I'm certain that they'd be glad to make the trip."

Out dashed the elves. And when Mickey Mouse had finished his cookies and milk beside the fire, they dashed back in with good news.

"Santa's old sleigh is waiting at the door, loaded with your Christmas mail," they said.

"We gave Santa a new sleigh as a surprise this year,"
Mrs. Santa Claus explained. "He's using it for the first
time tonight. Isn't that lucky? So the old one is here. And
the retired reindeer are all hitched up?"

"Yes," said the elves. "They're delighted to go. And two
of us will ride along to show the way."

So off went Mickey Mouse in Santa Claus's own
sleigh. And he and the elves flew faster than the wind,
behind those reindeer's flying heels.

They delivered all that Christmas mail before the night was old. And then the elves took Mickey Mouse home.

"Come back some time on a polar flight to pick up your plane," they said.

And Mickey promised that he would.

So if some of your Christmas mail last year was dropped down the chimney Christmas Eve, or blown in under the door, if some of it had a special look, now you know the reason why.